Green Light Readers
For the new reader who's ready to GO!

Amazing adventures await every young child who is eager to read.
   Green Light Readers encourage children to explore, to imagine, and to grow through books. Created for beginning readers at two levels of skill, these lively illustrated stories have been carefully developed to reinforce reading basics taught at school and to make reading a fun and rewarding experience for children and grown-ups to share outside the classroom.

   The grades and ages within each skill level are general guidelines only, and books included in both levels may feature any or all of the bulleted characteristics. When choosing a book for a new reader, remember that every child progresses at his or her own pace—be patient and supportive as the magic of reading takes hold.

1 **Buckle up!**
   Kindergarten–Grade 1: Developing reading skills, ages 5–7
   • Short, simple stories • Fully illustrated • Familiar objects and situations
   • Playful rhythms • Spoken language patterns of children
   • Rhymes and repeated phrases • Strong link between text and art

2 **Start the engine!**
   Grades 1–2: Reading with help, ages 6–8
   • Longer stories, including nonfiction • Short chapters
   • Generously illustrated • Less-familiar situations
   • More fully developed characters • Creative language, including dialogue
   • More subtle link between text and art

Green Light Readers incorporate characteristics detailed in the Reading Recovery model used by educators to assess the readability of texts through the end of first grade. Guidelines for reading levels for these readers have been developed with assistance from Mary Lou Meerson. An educational consultant, Ms. Meerson has been a classroom teacher, a language arts coordinator, an elementary school principal, and a university professor.

Published in collaboration with Harcourt School Publishers

The
Fox
and the
Stork

The
Fox

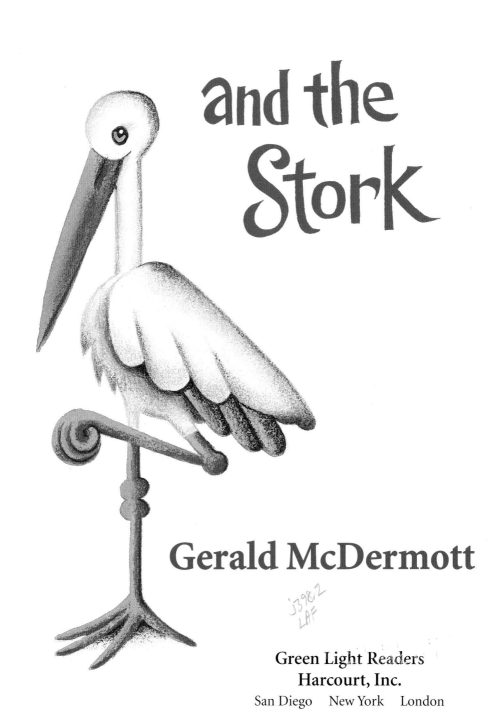

and the Stork

Gerald McDermott

Green Light Readers
Harcourt, Inc.
San Diego   New York   London

First Green Light Readers edition 1999
Green Light Readers is a registered trademark of Harcourt, Inc.

Library of Congress Cataloging-in-Publication Data
McDermott, Gerald.
The fox and the stork/Gerald McDermott.
p. cm.—(Green Light Readers)
Summary: A retelling of the La Fontaine fable in which a stork finds a way to
outwit the fox that tricked him.
[1. Fables. 2. Storks—Fiction. 3. Foxes—Fiction.] I. La Fontaine, Jean de,
1621–1695. II. Title. III. Series
PZ8.2.M15Fo 1999
[E]—dc21   98-55238
ISBN 0-15-202343-7
ISBN 0-15-202267-8 (pb)

B D F H J K I G E C
A C E G I J H F D B (pb)

Long ago, there was a fox who lived in the forest. Fox liked to play tricks on his friends.

One morning, Fox rowed his boat across the pond. He saw his friend Stork. "Would you like to come to my house for dinner?" he asked.

"How kind of you to ask!" said Stork.
"Yes, I would like that."

That night, Stork rowed her boat across the pond. She walked along the forest road. Then she tapped on Fox's door with her long bill.

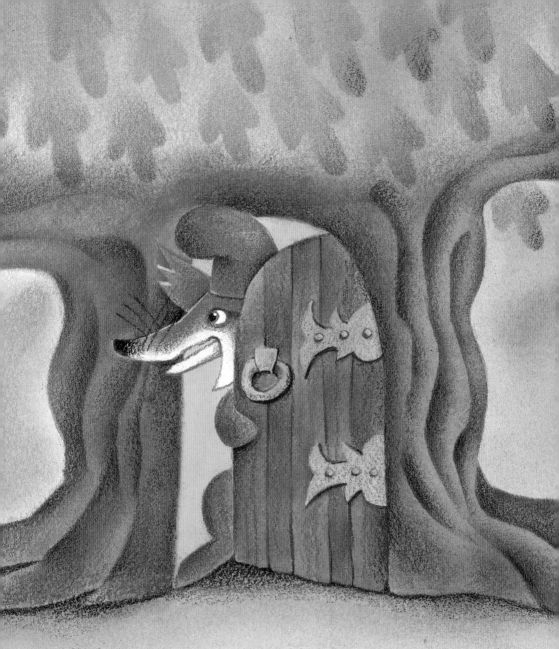

"Come in," said Fox. "I made soup!"
"I like soup," said Stork.

Fox and Stork sat down to eat. Fox didn't put the soup in a bowl. He served it on a flat dish.

Fox felt very smart. Stork couldn't eat
from the flat dish. All she could do was
dip the tip of her long bill into the soup.
Fox soon slurped it all up!

Stork was still hungry, but she didn't complain.
"Thank you for the dinner," said Stork.
"Come to my house, and I'll make dinner for you."

The next day, Fox rowed his boat to
Stork's house.

"I don't like to boast," said Stork, "but my soup is the best. I use greens that grow in my own garden."
"Wonderful! Let's eat!" said Fox.

Stork put the soup in a tall jar. Fox didn't get a drop. All he could do was lick the top of the jar. Stork dipped in her long bill and drank it all up.

Fox moaned as he rowed home. "I'm so hungry! This is my reward for tricking a friend!"

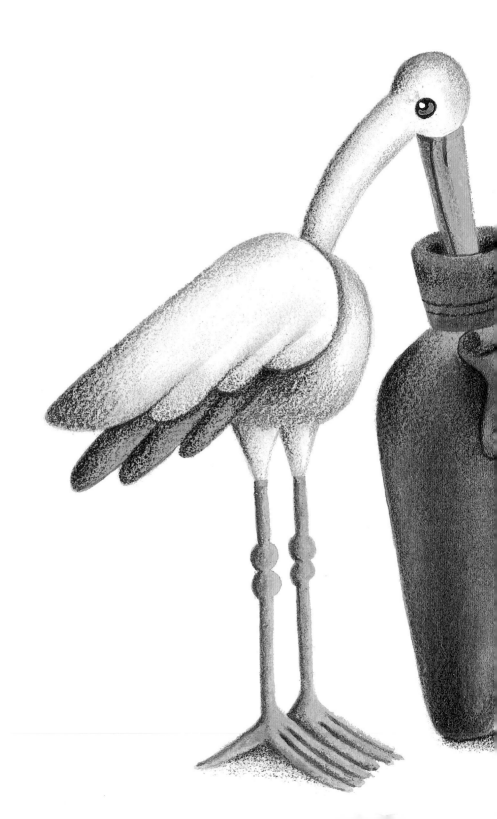

At last Fox saw that being kind to others is the right thing to do.

Meet the Author-Illustrator

Gerald McDermott likes to retell myths and folktales because these stories have special messages for people of all ages. He uses his pictures to help tell the story and get the message to his readers.

Gerald McDermott hopes that you enjoy reading **The Fox and the Stork** *as much as he did retelling it.*

Look for these other Green Light Readers—
all affordably priced in paperback!

Level 1/Kindergarten–Grade 1

Big Brown Bear
David McPhail

Cloudy Day/Sunny Day
Donald Crews

Down on the Farm
Rita Lascaro

Popcorn
Alex Moran
Illustrated by Betsy Everitt

Sometimes
Keith Baker

What I See
Holly Keller

Level 2/Grades 1–2

A Bed Full of Cats
Holly Keller

Catch Me If You Can!
Bernard Most

The Chick That Wouldn't Hatch
Claire Daniel
Illustrated by Lisa Campbell Ernst

I Wonder
Tana Hoban

Shoe Town
Janet Stevens and Susan Stevens Crummel
Illustrated by Janet Stevens

The Very Boastful Kangaroo
Bernard Most

Green Light Readers is a registered trademark of Harcourt, Inc.

Green Light Readers
For the new reader who's ready to GO!